DEDICATION

This book is dedicated to my daughter for her inspiration and input when writing the book, and anyone who has a wonder of the world.

The Hot Air Balloon

Delivered Some Cheese To The
Moon

So When He Comes Out Tonight

He Will Shine Extra Bright

We're All Waiting In The Park

And Now It's Getting Extra Dark

It's Glowing So Bright
Throughout The Park

Right On Time, And Never Too Soon

Here He Is,
It's Mr.moon!

He Says Hello,
It's Been A
While

And Lights Up The Sky With His
Smile

He's Happy And Thankful For The Cheese

From The Hot Air Balloon's
Deliveries

It's Time To Go, It's Getting Late

The Stars Are Out And Looking Great

The Moon Rises Up, And The
Stars All Follow

THE END

MEET THE AUTHOR

J.Mason is an independent children's author who started out writing books with, and for his daughter. This blossomed into a passion to create a shelf of rhyming happiness to share with the world.

J.Mason looks to create original books covering a wide array of subjects suitable for certain age groups. He wants to make reading books fun, whilst maintaining emotions specific to the subject.

J.Mason believes that the world is full of magic, and his aim is to capture it within his books.

Made in the USA
Las Vegas, NV
20 February 2024